The Twelve Days of Christmas

The Twelve Days of Christmas

A SONG REBUS

Illustrated by Emily Bolam

AN ANNE SCHWARTZ BOOK
ATHENEUM BOOKS FOR YOUNG READERS

Musical arrangement by Adam Stemple of "The Twelve Days of Christmas" from *Hark! A Christmas Sampler* by Jane Yolen, musical arrangements copyright © 1991 by Adam Stemple. Reprinted by permission of G. P. Putnam's Sons.

Atheneum Books for Young Readers
An imprint of Simon & Schuster Children's Publishing Division
1230 Avenue of the Americas
New York, New York 10020

Book design by Angela Carlino

The text of this book is set in Priska Serif.
The illustrations are rendered in acrylic paint.

First Edition
Printed in China for Harriet Ziefert, Inc.
10 9 8 7 6 5 4 3 2 1

Library of Congress Cataloging-in-Publication Data
Twelve days of Christmas (English folk song)
The twelve days of Christmas : a song rebus / illustrated by Emily Bolam.—1st ed.
p. cm.
"An Anne Schwartz book."
Summary: On each of the twelve days of Christmas, unusual or extravagant
gifts arrive from a young woman's true love.
ISBN 0-689-81101-2
1. Folk songs, English—England—Texts. 2. Christmas music. [1. Folk
songs, England. 2. Christmas music.] I. Bolam, Emily, ill. II. Title.
PZ8.3.T8517 1997
782.42'1723'00268
[E]—dc20   96-25147

Illustrator's Note

One year, I went to a Christmas party and someone suggested that we play a singing game, like the ones that were popular hundreds of years ago in England.

The rules of the game were explained. We would all pick numbers from a bowl. The person who picked number one would sing the first stanza of "The Twelve Days of Christmas." The next person would follow with the second stanza plus the original lines. And the next person would follow with the third stanza, plus remember the other two verses.

Since I am not very good at remembering the words to songs, I hoped for a low number. But I picked number nine. Goodness! I knew it would be difficult to remember the order of the eight gifts that went before the ninth one, which I thought was nine drummers drumming.

I sang in turn . . . but without help from the audience I never would have made it all the way back to the partridge.

When I got home that evening, I drew little pictures of lords, ladies, pipers, drummers, maids, swans, geese, rings, calling birds, hens, turtle doves, and, of course, the partridge. Then, using the pictures to help me remember, I sang a perfect rendition of "The Twelve Days of Christmas."

I dedicate this rebus book to everyone—grown-ups and children alike—whose singing is greatly improved when they don't have to remember the words!

Emily Bolam
Brighton, England

On the first day of Christmas
my true love gave to me
a partridge in a pear tree.

On the second day of Christmas
my true love gave to me
two turtle doves

and a in a pear tree.

On the third day of Christmas
my true love gave to me
three French hens

2

and a in a pear tree.

On the fourth day of Christmas
my true love gave to me
four calling birds

3

2

and a  in a pear tree.

On the fifth day of Christmas
my true love gave to me
five golden rings

4

3

2

and a  in a pear tree.

On the sixth day of Christmas
my true love gave to me
six geese a-laying

5

4

3

2

and a  in a pear tree.

On the seventh day of Christmas my true love gave to me seven swans a-swimming

6

5

4

3

2

and a 🐦 in a pear tree.

On the eighth day of Christmas
my true love gave to me
eight maids a-milking

7

6

5

4

3

2

and a  in a pear tree.

On the ninth day of Christmas
my true love gave to me
nine drummers drumming

8

7

6

5

4

3

2

and a  in a pear tree.

On the tenth day of Christmas
my true love gave to me
ten pipers piping

9

8

7

6

5

4

3

2

and a 🐦 in a pear tree.

On the eleventh day of Christmas
my true love gave to me
eleven ladies dancing

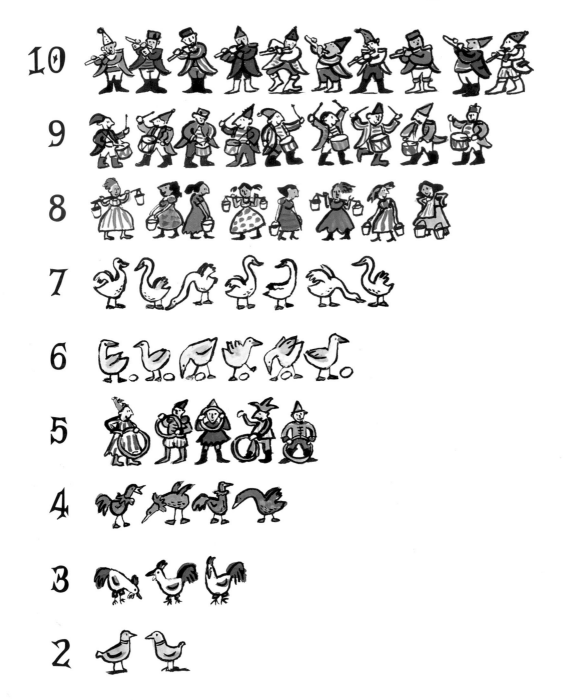

10

9

8

7

6

5

4

3

2

and a 🐦 in a pear tree.

On the twelfth day of Christmas my true love gave to me twelve lords a-leaping

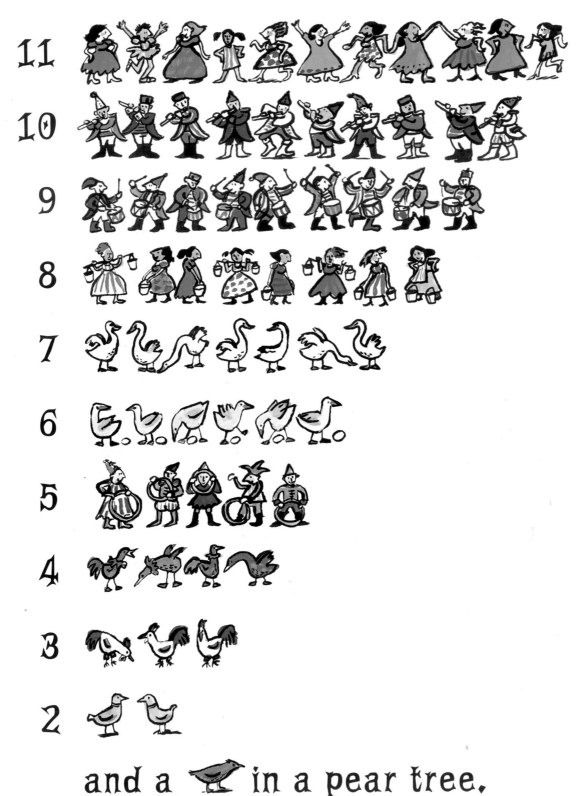

11

10

9

8

7

6

5

4

3

2

and a 🐦 in a pear tree.

The Twelve Days of

Christmas

true love gave to me five gold-en rings, four cal-ling birds,

three French hens, two_ tur-tle doves, and a par-tridge in a pear tree.

accumulative

D.S. al Fine

On the
{ sixth
seventh
eighth
ninth
tenth
eleventh
twelfth }
day of Christ-mas my true love gave to me
{ six geese a - lay - ing,
seven swans a - swim - ming,
eight maids a - milk - ing,
nine drum-mers drum - ming,
ten pip - ers pip - ing,
eleven la - dies danc - ing,
twelve lords a - leap - ing, }